D0607469

CALGARY PUBLIC LIBRARY

NOV   2014

CAROLYN BECK Illustrated by KAREN PATKAU

One
Hungry
Heron

Fitzhenry & Whiteside

Text © 2014 Carolyn Beck
Illustrations © 2014 Karen Patkau
5 4 3 2 1

All rights reserved. No part of this publication may be reproduced, stored in a retrieval system or transmitted, in any form or by any means, without the prior written permission of Fitzhenry & Whiteside or, in the case of photocopying or other reprographic copying, a licence from Access Copyright (Canadian Copyright Licensing Agency), 1 Yonge Street, Suite 800, Toronto, ON, M5E 1E5, fax (416) 868-1621.

Published in Canada by Fitzhenry & Whiteside, 195 Allstate Parkway, Markham, ON, L3R 4T8 www.fitzhenry.ca
Published in the U.S. by Fitzhenry & Whiteside, 311 Washington Street, Brighton, Massachusetts 02135

We acknowledge with thanks the Canada Council for the Arts, and the Ontario Arts Council for their support of our publishing program. We acknowledge the financial support of the Government of Canada through the Canada Book Fund (CBF) for our publishing activities.

Canada Council **Conseil des Arts**
for the Arts **du Canada**

ONTARIO ARTS COUNCIL
CONSEIL DES ARTS DE L'ONTARIO
an Ontario government agency
un organisme du gouvernement de l'Ontario

Library and Archives Canada Cataloguing in Publication
ISBN 978-1-55455-361-7 (bound)
Data available on file

Publisher Cataloging-in-Publication Data (U.S.)
ISBN 978-1-55455-361-7 (bound)
Data available on file

Text and cover design by Kong Njo
Cover illustration courtesy of Karen Patkau

Printed and bound in China by Sheck Wah Tong Printing Press Ltd.

To Flo, who taught me to see the small critters

—C.B.

For One and the Other One

—K.P.

One hungry heron,
tall and still,
crooks her leg
and tips her bill.

Two drowsy catfish,
way down deep,
snuffle through the muck,
then go to sleep.

Three darting dragonflies
hover and dip.
Whiz! Pause! Whiz!
Zoom! Zoom! Zip!

4

Four water walkers,
light as air,
skim, skitter, skate
there, here, there.

Five bustling beavers —
a building crew —
lug and tug
and chew, chew, chew!

Six slinky snakes
slither through the ferns.
They make curly kinks
and long twisty turns.

Seven gliding snails,
all in a line,
leave shiny trails
as they inch up a vine.

Eight hoppy frogs
with bulging eyes
soak and croak
and snap up flies.

Nine paddly ducks
dabble in the reeds.
They flap and quack
and snack on weeds.

Ten tiny turtles
looking for sun
perch on a log
one by one,
by one, by one,
by one, one, one,
one, one . . .
one.

Plip!
One little drip.
Then **two** plop-plops.
Three, **four**, **five**,
six big drops!
Seven and **eight**
splips and splats.
Nine, and **ten** pit-a-pat pats.

More and more
and more — even MORE!
What do you know?
It's starting to pour!

Rumble! Rumble!
10 turtles tumble.
9 ducks dip out of sight.

Thunder! Thunder!
8 frogs dive under.
7 snails curl up tight.

Pitter! Patter!
6 snakes scatter.
5 beavers scoot
to their lodge.

Crack! Crackle! Crash!
4 water walkers dash.
3 dragonflies dart and dodge.

Flick! Flicker! Flash!
2 catfish splash.
1 heron flaps to her tree.

Helter skelter!
They all find shelter.
Now there is not one to see.

0

Zero. Naught. None.
Till the storm is done.
Then they come
back again.

One, two, three, four, five, six, seven, eight, nine, and **ten**.